THE RISING SUN AT SHILONG

ABHRA BAPARY

Made with ♥ on the Notion Press Platform
www.notionpress.com

Contents

ONE

The Beginning

In 2005, a seven-year-old boy named Arjun found him-self at a family wedding, surrounded by cousins who teased him for not playing with them. "Hey, little boy, why aren't you staying with us tonight?" they chided.

The mood was joyous, the children were playful, but Arjun felt out of place. His parents decided to stay the night at a relative's house, where everyone enjoyed themselves—except for Arjun. He retreated into his own world, feeling isolated despite being surrounded by family. This was just one day in Arjun's life, but it was indicative of the many days that followed.

Fast forward twenty years to 2025,

Arjun, now an adult, was still the same quiet, introverted person. He had built a life around his routines, rarely venturing beyond the confines of his home. His mother often urged him to go outside, reminding him that life couldn't be lived through a screen.

"Arjun! Why don't you just go outside? It's not the way to be human!" his mother said one day, exasperated. "You're still the same old Arjun! Try to change this. You never involve yourself in our family life. Don't you think I've been going through a lot since your father passed away? You don't even go to the market anymore."

But Arjun was resistant. "What is new?" he replied. "I am like this. Why are you compelling me to go outside? I'm happy in my own world." As he said this, he was watching a travel blog about Shillong. His mother noticed and said, "Don't even think of going there!"

"Why should I go?" Arjun responded, more out of habit than curiosity.

His mother sighed, "You can, Arjun. You're brave. Don't worry about what the world thinks of you. You're just overthinking all the time. You just need to step outside and have the willpower." His mother left.

TWO

THE JOURNEY BEGINS

One month later, Arjun found himself on a journey he never thought he'd take. The Vande Bharat train from Siliguri to Guwahati saved him time and energy, making the trip as smooth as possible. However, he knew the road ahead, leading deeper into the hills, might test his endurance. After arriving at Guwahati station in the morning, Arjun saw a massive crowd moving along the platform in front of him. This was not his first experience, but he did not have his father by his side this time whose hand was there to protect him in that huddle. He slowly made his way towards the over bridge by pushing the crowd. While walking on the roadway of over-bridge he could watch the trains entering or leaving the station. Finally he got down from the over-bridge and went to the bus station where the Meghalaya Transport Corporation bus was standing still. He turned his phone on to see the bus number and rode the bus. He had already booked the ticket beforehand to make his journey hassle free. But he could not decide where to keep his luggage in the shelf or beside him. Him internally, “Somebody can snatch it if I went asleep. Should I leave it to there? No, I should keep it by my side.” He firstly kept it in his lap but shifted it to his side seat. But after 5 minute, a girl came and stood beside him. Seeing the number of her seat she said, “Could you please keep it aside?” But Arjun was not listening to her. He was listening to his earphone facing his head towards the floor of the car. So the girl had to touch her to wake him up which made an awkward situation for him. Seeing the stranger, he said, “Ha! What!” She said, “Is this your bag?” “Yes. Yes.” said Arjun. “So, can you please keep it aside?” said her. Arjun finally kept it in his lap again but could not handle it well and fell on the floor. Seeing uncomfortable with the bag, she told him “You can keep it in the shelf.” Arjun did not pay heed to that as he was okay with that situation whatever bad it felt may be. By the way, she was a backpacker and a frequent solo traveler from Kolkata, but unlike Arjun, she seemed at ease with the world around her. At 7:30 AM the bus set off for its destination. The sweet music of Garo tribe made the ambiance for the travelers. Dashing through the busy roads of Guwahati City, it finally entered to the Meghalaya state. The hilly roads conveyed that. The girl, Meera, didn’t say much at first. As Arjun, she too was a first-time visitor to Shillong and seemed content to gaze out the window as the bus made its way up the winding roads. After a while, Meera turned to Arjun and asked, "Can you please give me the window seat for a few moments? I have to vlog." The bright sunny day, with its cold breeze, made for ideal travel weather. The bus driver, a local, started a conversation with Meera, telling her that spring was the second-best season to visit Shillong after the rainy season. Meera eagerly asked him about the best places to visit, absorbing every detail. They noticed all the beautiful sceneries full of hills, beautiful forests, floras and little bit faunas. The majestic landscape of Umiam Lake in the midst of hills might attract them but not the foul smell of that lake. After an hour, the bus reached Police Bazar, and everyone disembarked. Meera went off to find a hotel, and Arjun, still somewhat hesitant, did the same. The day had passed, and though he felt a twinge of anxiety, Arjun knew he was in a different world now—a world far from his comfort zone.

THREE

The Nervous Morning

That morning, Arjun found himself at Shillong Peak, where he saw the landscape of Shillong City—a city nestled in the mountains. The foggy, breathtaking view captivated his soul. He had never imagined the world could look like this. He saw it previously through the screen but for the first time through his eyes. It felt like a new world was unveiling itself to him, expanding his horizons in ways he had never thought possible. As he stood there, capturing the scene on his phone, he realized that this Arjun was different from the one who would wake up at 10 a.m. and head straight to the office. This Arjun was seeing life through a new lens, one that offered beauty, excitement, and a sense of adventure.

"Hey! You're just seeing the first view," Meera said, noticing his amazement. "You're so amazed. I think you haven't imagined how many more views are waiting for you." She was also capturing the beauty of Shillong from the watchtower.

Meera then asked, "What's your plan now?" That was out of the world question not of Arjun's world. Arjun initially puzzled in his hesitative world. Guessing that she again reasserted, “Hey we shared the same bus in the early morning! Don’t you?” This time Arjun said, “yes. I do remember”.

Getting response, she again asked, “So, where are you heading?” Arjun slowly began to unfurl his wings. "I’m heading to Elephant Falls," Arjun replied.

"Really? I think we can both share the travel. I’m also going that way. How many days are you planning to stay?"

"Two days," Arjun answered, still hesitant but feeling Meera’s enthusiasm rubbing off on him.

Meera smiled. "Why not make this a shared journey? Are you going to Cherrapunji?""Yes," Arjun nodded. In that moment, Arjun thought it might be good to have some company. Maybe Meera wasn’t a harmful stranger after all. So, shared journey began.

FOUR

ELEPHANT FALLS

They hired a car with the first destination to Elephant Falls and then Canyon and so on. They both sat on the rear seat. But Arjun kept his big luggage in between them while Meera kept it in the front seat as it was vacant. Meera asked the driver, "Bhaiya, firstly we are going to local sights and then u can go to Cherapunji. And whatever we decided about the expense with you, we have no problem. We agree to that." Arjun nodded his head. The driver said, "No problem. But we have to leave for Cherapunji before 4 PM from the canyon. You know it is a hilly area so we have to reach their early." Meera was excited to go to the Elephant falls. The sight has three falls and each has its own beauty. First fall is above then 2nd fall can be seen after walking down the steps and finally the 3rd fall. After the driver parked the car, Meera started blogging seeing and hearing those sounds of water fall. This has amazed Arjun also. The sound seems so sweet that Arjun ran towards it. Meera was blogging saying, "Look where we are, The majestic Elephant Falls, the murmuring sounds of the fountain is so soothing, you just cannot describe it through phone".

Arjun in his mind "How it can be so majestic, it is just a fall, it is not angels or Victoria".

Then after seeing all those falls they ascended the way by which they got down and finally rested on a bench put there. Arjun was heavily panting and he could hear his heartbeat. Meera was also same but little bit less. Meera said, "It is just the beginning. Btw I did not ask you, your name?"

"I am Arjun", he said. "Nice! I am Meera." They hand shook while panting.

"Arjun, btw where are you from?" asked Meera.

Hesitating a little bit, "I am from Siliguri. You?"

"I am from Yadavpur, Kolkata. So, Arjun, What is next?" Meera said.

"The canyon", Arjun said.

"yes! How we can miss that. It is majestic. Lets go".

FIVE

THE MAJESTIC CANYON

Arjun and Meera continued their journey to Shillong Canyon before heading to Cherrapunji. When they arrived at the canyon, they were both awestruck by its majesty. They were hungry after the trip, and as they sat on a bench, Meera asked, "Aren't you feeling hungry? The driver said we have two hours here before we head to Cherrapunji. It's already 3:00 PM, so we should start soon."Despite their hunger, the canyon's beauty held their attention. Meera, with her infectious enthusiasm, ran toward the edge, careful enough not to get too close to the drop. The temperature was cool, making the adrenaline rush even more exhilarating for her. Arjun, on the other hand, moved slowly and cautiously, but seeing Meera's excitement piqued his own interest. As he approached Meera from behind, he couldn't help but be amazed by the view. "I've never seen anything like this before," Meera said, her voice filled with awe. Arjun felt the same. Meera then asked, "Hey Arjun, can you please hold the camera for a moment?" "Sure, no problem," Arjun replied. He had become more lenient, shedding some of his previous self-centeredness. Meera started talking to the camera, "Look where we are! It is so beautiful, breathtaking u just cannot imagine. Arjun, can you bring the camera closer to the canyon? Look at what's behind us. It's Shillong Canyon. It's so deep that if I threw a stone, it would probably fly right over it. Arjun, please give the camera back—I want to show the landscape." Meera asked Arjun to capture some moments of her in that place. She was giving some poses on the railing made of bamboos. Arjun saw her first time through the mobile phone camera. But no attraction for her at that moment. After strolling down the white earthy roads for more than 1 hour they almost forgot that they had been starving since morning. "Oh! I almost forgot that I am hungry", said Meera. They searched for food and they did not have to wait for any longer. They enjoyed some momos and cylindrical papads, savoring the flavors as much as the experience.

SIX

THE JOURNEY TO CHERRAPUNJI

After exploring Shillong Canyon, Arjun and Meera continued their journey towards Cherrapunji. The scenic drive through the hills was a fresh experience for Arjun, a stark contrast to his previous life confined to his room and office. Despite his lingering anxiety, he felt a sense of adventure stirred by Meera's enthusiasm. They arrived in Cherrapunji in the late afternoon. Meera was still buzzing with excitement and documented their travels in her blog. As they reached their hotel near Eco Park, the evening was settling in. They decided to have dinner at the hotel, which consisted of egg and rice. When the hotel lady asked if they needed one room, Arjun responded, "Actually, we need two." Meera chimed in with a smile, "We're not together; we're just traveling together." The hotel lady nodded, understanding the situation. They ordered their food rice, chicken and egg fry.

After entering his room Arjun went to the bathroom to check whether it is in good state or not. Then after putting off his clothes and wearing on some fresh ones he lied on his bed looking at the above ceiling. Actually, he needed to reflect the day which felt like a year. He never enjoyed this much companion of someone except his one or two friends. Pondering the thoughts he felt asleep until the moment when Meera called on him and knocked on his door. Meera said, "The food is ready, and the lady already returned from your door. By the way, give me your number, otherwise I cannot contact you." So many words for Arjun, obviously made him irritated as he just woke up from sleep. By the way Arjun gave her his mobile number. And then they went to the dining table to eat their dinner. They enjoyed their dinner and then settled in for the night, preparing for the next day's exploration.

SEVEN

DISCOVERING ECO PARK

The next morning, Arjun went early, unusual from his daily routine from Siliguri. Actually he already slept a lot before the dinner the previous day. So he went outside opening the door. But he saw Meera was already outside. The sound of flip flop of Arjun , made Meera turned to him. Seeing Arjun Meera said, “Hey! come here.” She was throwing pieces of biscuits to the birds. “Do you do this every day?”, Meera said. “Yes! I do that every morning. Oh! I forgot that the ecopark is siatuted very near to it. The driver has said yesterday. Lets go there.” “Hey! I am wearing flip flap.”“So what! We are not running. Btw running may cause harm to you,” said Meera with a cheeky smile. Then they went to visit Eco Park. Located up in the hills, they followed a winding road through a valley dotted with small hills and cemeteries. As they approached Eco Park, Meera reflected on the previous night’s view from her room. "The night view was so paranormal. I really enjoyed it." Eco Park, though smaller compared to Shillong Canyon, offered its own charm. They strolled through the park, soaking in the tranquil environment and the cool morning air. Upon reaching the park, Meera started walking alongside the railing at the side of a small canyon. “Something is interesting about it. Can you guess?” Meera asked Arjun. Arjun remembering the memory of the blogs of Shilong said, “But the weather is foggy. You cannot see it. But there is a place where we can see it.”After returning from the park, they took breakfast and then they headed towards Nohkalikai Waterfalls, the famous waterfall of Shilong.

EIGHT

The Nohkalikai Waterfalls

After reaching the waterfall, Meera as usual started her blogging and Arjun was slowly coming to the edge of the canyon to see the great Nohkalikai waterfalls. This was one of the best memories that were going to remain in his brain for the rest of his life. The foamy white water could be seen from the edge of railing. So many people were photo shooting for their memories to be kept for future with this water fall. Arjun was little bit different he was only seeing this scenery. For him this scenery was to be felt live not to be felt in future through photos. But who knew his mind. Someone asked him to photograph a picture of a group who came from South India. Arjun did not say no.

Meera slightly different from her previous blogging, started blogging, "Just hear those fountain waters falling on those rocks, it gives you the vibe of heaven. May be heaven is not so different." She said those in a light tone. They were enjoying those sceneries so much that 2 hours just passed until their driver reminded them that they had more places to visit.

While going to the Double Decker root bridge, they stopped for The Seven Sister Falls for some moments to blog only for Meera. Meera could not miss those chance to blog those famous places.

NINE

The Trek to the Double Decker Bridge

After their visit to the Seven Sister Water Falls, Arjun and Meera set off for the Double Decker Living Root Bridge. This day is looking lively and Meera was lively and excited too, blogging about their destination. "We're heading to the Living Root Bridge, the world-famous bridge. I'm so excited!" The trek to the Double Decker Bridge was about 5 km, contrary to Arjun's initial estimate of 1 km. As they began the ascent, Arjun was taken aback by the distance and the steep climb. "I thought it was just 1 km," he said, feeling a bit overwhelmed. Meera, undeterred, encouraged him. "Why are you over thinking? Let's go!" She grabbed his hand, urging him forward. Arjun hesitated but then agreed. "Okay, let's do it." During the trek, Arjun found himself struggling. His heart raced, and he needed to take breaks frequently. At one point, Meera noticed his fatigue and suggested a rest. "Let's take a break. We've covered quite a bit of distance already." After resting, they continued their trek. Despite the challenge, Arjun was struck by the beauty and tranquility of the surroundings. He reflected on how different and more vibrant this world seemed compared to his previous, more confined existence. Finally, after three more stops, they reached the Double Decker Bridge. The sight was breathtaking, and the effort of the trek was worth it. Arjun felt a deep sense of accomplishment and awe, realizing that this journey was opening his eyes to new experiences and possibilities. At the top at the Double Decker bridge, they were completely awed seeing the beauty of the so called natural landscape. Arjun was crossing the bridge and Meera was behind him blogging the scenery and then Arjun turned behind seeing the same Meera with his mobile phone, she was glistering in the sun from the canopy of trees. There are thousands of species of trees but this tree has made itself so famous. Otherwise who remember a tiny specie in the world of humans.

The cryptic natural landscape might lighten Arjun's inner world with a happy ambiance. The panting was forgotten the rough steps left his mind, but one thing was always in his mind the thought of going to miss those lively moments in his bedroom in his world in future. But they had to leave the place because they had to visit two more places, Arwah Cave and Mawsmai Cave.

TEN

RETURNING TO SHILONG

After visiting their travelling destinations, they finally have to return to the Shilong city. They were more comfortable in discussing about their personal things. Actually they could not find that much spare time in these two days except that day. Arjun asked Meera, “So! Meera what do you do for living?” Hesitating to say forward, she said, “What do you think I actually do? Okey! I am a blogger only!” “Really? ”Arjun asked. “I have done my B.Tech in Mechanical Engineering and now full time blogger. That is all. Btw what is about you?”

“I am a govt employee in Disaster Management”

“Oh! Then it is good to have you in these risky roads of Meghalaya”, chuckled Meera.

Arjun also chuckled. “So Arjun, you are from Siliguri, have you gone to Darjeeling?” “Yes! But very long ago”, said Arjun. “What! If I were in your place, I would go there every possible weekend. Actually I had gone there last year.”said Meera.

Soon, the car reached Shilong at Police Bazar More. Both got down from the car and they paid the charges to the driver. Finally it is time to say good bye. The queen of hills, might not seemed to be as crowded as Arjun's thoughts. It is so lonely in the night to say good bye to a person who has been his companion for two days. But Arjun while saying good bye to Meera, could not asked her to give her contacts because he was so preoccupied with other thoughts. Arjun only asked , "So, when will these two birds going to meet again?" Meera chuckled and answered, "May be some day somewhere! You are so changed now. Not the same Arjun anymore."

Meera said "Btw! Good Bye!"

"Bye", Arjun said with little bit weight in his voice. Arjun went to the same Hotel where he previously stayed. On his bed, Arjun was thinking about the moments, he would never forget. He only went out that night for food and then came back to sleep and he had to wake up early to come back to Guwahati to catch the train at 2 PM.

ELEVEN

THE HOMECOMING

At 9 AM in the morning he got up in the bus of Meghalaya Transport Corporation and was adjusting his luggage a bag pack at the shelf, a man was just sitting by side said, "you can keep it beside you, because not many persons are going to board this bus." "Why?" asked Arjun?

"This is morning bus. Shilong does not have many people like Kolkata."

The person was living in Shilong. The person was actually a non –meghalaya person. He was a person from Kolkata. He was living there in his wife's parental home. He had a house in Bangalore also. But this place attracts him a lot. The middle aged person was also a great story teller. He said Arjun to sit beside him because he was also a Bengali. Two Bengalis in Shilong running into is not an uncommon thing. Arjun could not but sit beside him. The person was telling him his story of his family and about his daughter who was a little bit different from him in sociablity. Actually she is like Arjun. That is why the person named Koushik was having so interest in him. They were telling their stories happily. Like Arjun said all about his travel throughout shilong. He also said about Meera.

"That is what I am saying Travelling is very good for health and mind. You will meet so many persons and enjoy their companion."

"Btw don't you love someone?" asked the person.

"No", said Arjun. "Don't mind! Actually I am asking because I have a daughter of your age. And she is always talking with her boyfriend. I don't mind this thing. Afterall it is her own life own decision", said the person. Arjun was silence.

"Actually you should have a love. I love my wife. There is something in the world which attracts us wherever we may be now. It may be telepathy, or it may be choices or it may be love for someone."

Arjun was listening to his words. And then in his mind thinking "I should have said her to give me her number. Whatever I have to find her, I have to say her something that I wanted to say but could not".

He also thanked her for bringing this much change in his life in his thought. He is now a free bird. He needs to fly more. After all it may be telepathy, or may be call.

www.ingramcontent.com/pod-product-compliance
Lightning Source LLC
LaVergne TN
LVHW041307150826
845673LV00008B/2774

* 9 7 9 8 8 9 6 7 3 0 5 5 2 *